Evergreen

A DRYAD'S TALE
& Other Short Stories

Sara Goodwin

Copyright © 2022 Sara Goodwin

All rights reserved. No part of this book may be reproduced in any form without the written permission of the publisher, except as permitted by U.S. copyright law.

This is a work of fiction. Names, characters, places, and incidents are products of the author's imagination or are used fictitiously. Any resemblance to actual events or persons, living or dead, is entirely coincidental.

ISBN: 979-8-218-01371-4

Book cover and interior design by E. McAuley:
www.emcauley.com

This book of stories is dedicated to my friends and family who have consistently put up with my nonsense for years on end. I love you people. So much.

Spring

Spring Dance

"There isn't much dignity in the forest in spring," said Winston the Gnome as he sat atop a large mushroom beside his brother Grinston.

"Nope," said Grinston, frowning as two birds flew by in a flash of bright feathers.

"Saw those two featherbrained fools in the meadow, doing the most ridiculous dance I ever saw. Heads bobbing everywhere, preening and fluffing their feathers! Meanwhile, the lady birds just sat on a branch, watching and tweeting."

"Silliness," said Grinston.

"Agreed," said Winston.

After a few moments had passed, Winston fished a small mirror out of his pocket and began to meticulously groom his beard, which grew to a well-manicured point at his chin. Grinston did the same.

The two gnomes rested in silence for a short while and soon began to snore.

A great crashing sound awakened them with a snorting start. In the clearing, two rams stood facing each other, pawing the ground. They ran toward each other, slamming their heads together with a mighty crack.

Winston grimaced. "Look at those fools! All of that effort to impress the ewes, and they're barely even paying attention!"

He motioned to where the ewes stood on the sideline, munching on grass while the rams competed for their favor. The younger of the two rams reared up on his hind legs and charged again, but the older ram easily brushed him to the side.

"Hare-brained beasts! They'll crack their heads open in their ridiculous display!" Grinston shook his head disapprovingly.

"Silliness," said Winston.

"Agreed," said Grinston, with a *harrumph*.

The two gnomes squinted up to take a look at the sun. It was getting quite late in the afternoon, and the brothers had been waiting for quite a long while.

"Do you think she's run into trouble?" Grinston asked.

Winston frowned. "It's well past four, and I thought we were to meet Griselda and Winona here, at these mushrooms, at three."

The brothers stood up and stretched, jogging in place for a brief moment to wake themselves up. Just then, they heard a slight rustling and a soft giggle from the shrubbery to their right.

Spring Dance

"It's the ladies! They're here! Quick, Grinston—does my new yellow vest make me look like an affluent gnome in his prime?"

Grinston nodded. "Of course, Brother! And what of my green vest?"

Winston agreed. "Like the green of spring's first leaves!"

Griselda and Winona arrived to meet their dates for the Gnomish Daffodil Festival dressed in yellow and green skirts with matching vests and blouses.

"Why, you look like daffodils yourselves, ladies!" Winston complimented them with a smile.

"Yes, lovely spring flowers, daffodils," said Grinston.

Griselda smiled at Grinston. "I must say, dear fellow, that your beard is resplendent this fine day! And the way your green vest looks just like a new leaf!" She blushed prettily and leaned in to kiss his cheek. The gnomes linked arms and walked toward the festival, laughing and talking all the way.

Winona planted a kiss on Winston's cheek and exclaimed that his yellow vest brought to mind the loveliest of the daffodils the forest had to offer. Linking arms, they followed the other gnomish couple toward the lights of the festival.

When the gnomes had gone, a rumpled, fluffy-feathered bird landed atop Winston's mushroom, and another alighted on Grinston's. The first bird shook his feathers out and made a bird-y grimace of disgust.

"There really isn't much dignity in the forest in spring," he said to the other bird, who nodded in agreement.

"Nope. Man, I'm exhausted from all of that dancing! I'm not even sure the lady birds even noticed me out there!"

The first bird shook his head. "It could be worse. At least we don't have beards!"

Summer

There Are Faeries in the Rose Garden

IF MAGIC WEREN'T IMPOSSIBLE, Iris would have sworn that she'd seen a tiny, humanoid man with wings land on the rose bush she was tending. If she hadn't been completely certain that there was no such thing as a faerie, she would never have been able to ignore the small, yellow-winged gentleman who stood on a rosebud watching her work.

The dilemma occurred when the... *hallucination* cleared his throat expectantly and said quite clearly, "I'm sorry to bother you, miss, but could I trouble you for a thimble? Silver, if you have it."

Iris stared but said nothing, the pruning shears falling to the ground with an ungainly thump.

The man wore tiny brown boots, a blue tunic, and green breeches the color of a leaf. His brown hair shone in the afternoon sun, and his handsome face bore an expression of frustration and impatience.

"Your mouth is open, dear lady. Pray, close it so that bugs might not find their way in. Have you a thimble?"

9

This time Iris managed to reply, "You're not possible!"

He grinned. "But I am. My name is Kelian, and I need your help! Again I ask: Have you a silver thimble?"

Iris nodded. "I'll have to go inside. It's in the hall closet. It was my grandmother's."

"Thank you! You won't regret it!"

Inside, Iris dug frantically through the sewing basket that had been her grandmother's. She found the silver thimble, and hurried back to the garden, her mind buzzing with both curiosity and alarm as she ran. *There is no such thing as a faerie! There is not a tiny man on a rose in my garden. Oh, Iris! You were out in the sun too long, and you're seeing things!*

But no, there he was. A tiny figure in blue and green, yellow wings twitching a bit with impatience. Iris knelt so that her face was at eye level with—with *Kelian*. The faerie. Who had a name and needed her thimble for something.

"Here." She held out the thimble and he took it. In his tiny hands it looked like a large bucket. "What do you need it for?"

He took a small packet from his pocket, dumped the ingredients into the thimble, and then held it out to catch a few droplets of water left over from Iris' very recent watering of the rosebush. The drops rolled from the petals and collected in the silver thimble, where they mixed with the contents of the packet to create a liquid of a magnificent, glowing blue. It looked like the sky, in liquid form, in a tiny thimble. Iris stared dumbly as he plunged his head into the thimble, drinking like her Aunt Daisy's jowly, old schnauzer on a hot day.

After a moment he came up for air, and Iris, quite comfortable in her newfound insanity where faeries were real and thimbles glowed, asked calmly, "Are you all right?"

Kelian offered her a sheepish grin. "I am now, thanks to your quick assistance. I had been poisoned, you see, and the antidote works best when brewed inside a silver thimble."

Her hand flew involuntarily to her throat, and she cried, "Poisoned?"

Kelian nodded gravely. "Poisoned. Octavia the Spider Queen had a few of my subjects trapped in her venomous web. In the process of defeating her, I was quite poisoned, I'm afraid. Though now you've saved my life, and I owe you a favor."

Still a bit shocked, Iris stammered, "Subjects? Favor?"

"By the gods, you are a strange creature," Kelian said. "I'm a faerie prince, and my subjects were in peril. You came to my rescue, and now I owe you a favor. What would you like? Gold? True love? Immortality?"

Iris narrowed her hazel eyes. "True love? Immortality? You can... do that?"

"Nope," Kelian said. "I was just teasing about those. True love is tricky, and immortality is no way to live."

At this Iris laughed. "I wouldn't have wanted those things anyway. I was just curious. You know, my grandmother believed in faeries. She told me stories about faeries when I was small, and as I got older, it became a bit of a joke between us. She knew I didn't really believe, but she appreciated that I pretended for her. I can only imagine what she would think if she were here now to see this!"

"She'd tell you that there are faeries in the rose garden, and that Prince Kelian is a dashing fellow, if a bit uncoordinated when suffering the effects of spider venom."

Iris' brow furrowed in concern. "Are you sure you're all right? The antidote worked? And what about your subjects? Are they well? And this - this Octavia. Is she still alive?"

The perennially charming smile the faerie prince wore slipped a little bit. "So many questions! And here I thought that humans were depressingly un-curious creatures! Not Iris Green—curiosity is your middle name, my dear!"

She blushed a little bit. "Well? Are you all right?"

"Right as rain, after the antidote. Though it will probably take me a bit to get my wings working again," he said as he shook his wings experimentally. "My subjects were freed by my lieutenant as I fought Octavia. They're quite all right. And as for the spider queen… let's just say she may have to change her name to Quinta after the harrying I gave her."

Iris shuddered. She had never cared much for spiders.

"So, if you are a prince, what am I to call you? May I refer to you simply as Kelian, or is a more formal title in order?"

He waved a hand in a careless gesture of nonchalance. "Just Kelian. Please."

"Very well, Kelian. May I ask how it is that you know my name? Only a moment ago, you called me Iris."

The faerie prince sat down on the rose petals, drawing his knees up to his chin, flexing his yellow wings. "I suppose it's because your grandmother told me so."

Iris clutched the engraved locket that she wore around her neck as she always did when she thought of her grandmother. She smiled. "So, when she was forever telling me that there were faeries in the rose garden, she was speaking from personal experience?"

Kelian nodded. "Violet's blackberry pie was legendary in Faerie. She would always leave a slice for us in the rose garden. We were great friends, Violet and I, and many others of my kind would call her friend as well. She saved my life with that very thimble the first time I met her, when she was no older than you are now." He flushed a bit. "Not that I'm always being poisoned or anything. The first time, it was Scorpius the Pincher-King. An unpleasant business altogether."

Iris remembered being very small and going with her grandmother with a single piece of blackberry pie to leave in the garden "for the faeries." She had humored her grandmother out of love, but she had never dreamed there were actually faeries in the garden looking forward to that slice of pie the way Iris herself always had! The idea was oddly comforting, especially now that her grandmother was gone.

She smiled at Kelian mischievously. "You know, I do have her recipe book. How would you and your friends like a feast of pie in honor of Grandmother Violet?"

The look on Kelian's face was like a child's on Christmas Eve, looking forward to Christmas Day with such intensity that sleep was impossible. "That would be a fitting tribute to Violet's memory, and to the forging of a new friendship as well! As soon as I can fly, I'll tell the others!" He studied Iris intently for a moment. "There is still the matter of your favor. What, short of love and immortality, can I do for you to express my gratitude?"

Iris had an idea, but was unsure he'd be able or willing to assist her. "I'm in a unique position, Kelian. I don't have a child or a husband, nor a passion for any career other than gardening. I lived here with my grandmother until she became ill, and I cared for her until she passed away. Any friends I had here have long moved away and started families of their own. I have a very strange request, and if it can't be done with faerie magic, then I can accept that, but I have to ask—"

Nodding, Kelian encouraged her to continue. "Please, tell me. If I can, then I will."

She took a deep breath, and said, "There's no more money to maintain the cottage and the garden. Men will come for it in a week and take it to be sold to the bank. There was never much money in selling herbs, remedies, and flowers for a living, as I discovered after my grandmother's passing. I want you to - to shrink the house and the garden and - and me. I want to keep doing as I do now for as long as possible, and the only way that can happen is if - if you make us a part of your world."

When the faerie prince did nothing but stare, Iris felt her heart drop to the toes of her shoes. She knew that it was too much, too strange a request. She'd only just discovered that faeries were real, and already she was making assumptions about how faerie magic worked! How silly he must think her!

"You want—to be like me? With - with wings? And the cottage and garden resized to match?"

She nodded. "If you can't, it's really all right. I - I was just overcome with *possibility* where there hadn't been any before."

"You're certain that's what you want? Absolutely certain?"

Iris nodded emphatically. "You mean it *is* possible? I could be like you? And keep the cottage and garden? If it can be, that's what I want more than anything else—more than gold, or or love, or money, or, well, anything!"

Kelian's smile was radiant. "Possible? Definitely. Preferable? Quite. And done? It nearly is. Hold out your hand to me."

She did as he asked, and he emptied the silver thimble of the remnants of the antidote, pushing the thimble onto her finger. He spoke in a language that was foreign to Iris and silver runes glowed on her hand and then on the petals of the rose he stood upon. She felt an odd, tugging sensation, and everything went dark. For a moment, she was afraid something had gone terribly wrong and she'd been blinded; but then she heard Kelian call her name and felt a hand grasp hers. A hand that was the same size as her own.

Iris allowed the hand to guide her, and blinked as the sunlight dazzled her eyes. Before her stood Kelian, a look of contrition on his face. "I didn't think. Your wings formed first and somehow that caused your dress to not, um, *change* with the rest of you. Magic is tricky like that sometimes."

Looking down, she realized she was no longer clothed and gave a shriek of surprise. Kelian quickly used his sword to cut a rough bolt of material from her fallen dress. He didn't peek while she hastily formed a sort of toga out of the cloth. It was harder than it should have been because she wasn't used to having wings in the way of her dressing activities.

Wings! She looked over her shoulder to see them, and gave a squeak of excitement when she saw they were a deep purple, feathered like a butterfly's wings, just like Kelian's.

"Is - is it what you wanted? Are you happy with it?" Kelian's voice sounded hopeful, like a child who'd made a drawing for a parent and wanted it to be displayed proudly.

She found she couldn't stop smiling. "Purple! I love them!"

"Iris colors for Iris." He shrugged. "It only seemed right."

Looking around her, she realized she couldn't see the house or the garden. Before she could even voice the question, Kelian answered her concern. "The cottage and garden are deep in the forest, in my kingdom. We can go there—I'll teach you to fly on the way!"

Iris moved her wings back and forth, feeling the pull of unfamiliar muscles in her shoulders and back. When she looked down, she saw her feet were hovering above the grass. *Iris, an hour ago you didn't believe in faeries and now you are one yourself!* She laughed, beating her wings faster and faster until she was able to rise even higher.

"I'm flying, Kelian! I'm *flying*!"

He flew up to join her and took her hands. "I should certainly hope so! I did make you a faerie." But his face lit up with happiness as much as hers did. "Shall we go and see about your cottage? I certainly hope the recipe book with the blackberry pie was inside the house when I shrank it."

As she flew away with Kelian toward the cottage with the rose garden, the only home she had ever known, she began to suspect that even though Kelian had told her he couldn't grant her love with his magic, she'd found it nonetheless.

Excerpts from the Tales of Kelian the Faerie Prince

As told to Captain Jonathan Calendar

1.)

Lord Kelian the Brave beneath a bluebell stood
To shelter from the rain and use the flower as a hood.
When his tiny bride flew near, riding on a bird,
She laughed and stole his bright blue hat, and said it looked absurd.

Against the goblins, orcs, and giants, Kelian stood strong.
He led his troops with valor against the evil throng.
He kept them out of Faerie, and out of the Sacred Vale,
And for these deeds he won the favor of the Age-Old Snail.

The dragons were in trouble, beset by packs of howls.
The ancient creatures needed help and asked the King of Owls.
The Owl King sent for Kelian and his Company of Light,

And that is why the dragons have great respect for one so slight.

Lord Kelian stood face to eye with the Warlord of the North.
The enemy laughed and shook his head when Kelian's army sallied forth.
"Ho, there, tiny Captain," the warlord teased and mocked,
And then he found he was on the ground—off his feet he had been knocked.

Lord Kelian's faerie lady, no bigger than a thumb,
Alighted right beside him on a branch of a great sweetgum.
She asked him, "Would you like to race? To fly with me, my sweet?"
He smiled and said, "Flying yes, but racing no; because, my dear, you cheat!"

2.)

Of Kelian the Brave a tale is told
About his battles brave and bold.

Crown Prince of Faerie in a world of Men,
He helped save the world over and over again.

With yellow wings and nut-brown hair,
None as lovely as he was found anywhere.

Excerpts from the Tales of Kelian the Faerie Prince

He sacrificed much to do his part,
To keep Faerie safe and preserve its art.

Among his best friends were those of all races,
From humans and centaurs and those with horned faces.

Commanding his troops who fly fast on the wing,
He flew with the dragons to fight on Mount Sing.

So brave was he there that the dragons they named him,
"The small one who fights with the force of ten strong men."

Autumn

In the Reflection

"The frogs know both of you, on either side of the reflection. They live in the reflection and can hop ashore to see how both of you are doing." —Darius (the) Green

When Prince Darius the Green, so called because of his love of nature, ran afoul of Naida the Water Witch, her perverse sense of humor caused her to turn him into a frog.

"Now," she cackled manically, "now you truly are Darius the Green!"

Darius watched in horror as his skin turned green and his soft clothing crumpled to the ground. He had to wriggle his way out of his own boot, through his pant leg, and out the top of his trousers just to escape.

Naida reached for him and held him up at eye level. "You'll stay a frog for all eternity unless you can convince some poor fool to kiss you."

He tried to speak, but could only croak. He tried again and managed to navigate his new vocal cords enough to say, "Kind of a cliché, don't you think, Naida?"

She narrowed her eyes in a threatening scowl. "Not cliché. Tried and true. It's going to be harder than you think,

Romeo. Most people don't want to put their lips on a slippery green frog, and many others are put off by talking creatures. And just any old kiss won't work. It has to be a kiss of good faith. Good luck finding that in this day and age!"

With that, Naida tossed him into the pond and disappeared in a puff of blue smoke.

Darius was relieved his frog's body seemed to have some instinct of its own when it came to swimming, but it was still difficult to get used to being small, naked, and green when he had been accustomed to being tall, well clothed, and not green. He supposed he'd been vain, but that hardly seemed crime enough to warrant being turned into a frog. Naida was angry with him for helping the beavers—who had moved into the stream—block the flow of the water. When he'd refused to dismantle the dam, she'd tried to convince him in *other* ways. Naida was beautiful, but she wasn't kind, and Darius had spurned her advances.

And, he thought mopily, *that ended in:* green.

Time passed slowly. He found he could understand many of the creatures of the forest. The beavers whose dam had caused his hardship felt terrible about his plight. Mrs. Beaver visited nearly every day and fretted over him. She worried constantly that he would be picked off by an Eagle if he sat atop a rock or lily pad for too long. Her sister had nearly lost a kit that way and the family had been extra vigilant ever since. Mr. Beaver brought him food and sat with him as Darius wrapped his mind around his increasing desire to eat bugs. Previously he'd been a vegetarian.

"The missus and I are vegetarians, but we find lots of bugs in our dam. Here, have some nasty—I mean *tasty*—dead flies. Killed 'em myself just moments ago." Mr. Beaver proudly grinned his bucktoothed grin. "Smacked 'em with my tail."

Darius eyed the flies suspiciously, then surprised himself as his long tongue darted out to catch them. For a moment, the idea of eating flies nearly caused him to be sick and he imagined he must be turning greener. Then he felt a strange, satisfied feeling in his gut. He was a frog. Frogs ate flies. *He* ate flies.

"Thank you," said Darius. "That was strangely delicious in the very worst way."

Mr. Beaver gave him a concerned glance. "The missus says you're to stay out of the open. Eagles, you know."

Darius nodded. "Sounds like a terrible way to die. Assure your wife I will do my best to stay clear of Eagles."

It was in his first year as a frog that Darius discovered the Other Place. At least, that was what the other frogs called it. A fat, old bullfrog by the name of Reginald explained that when humans and other land-dwelling creatures saw reflections in the water, they were actually seeing into the Other Place. According to Reginald, the Other Place was a lot like this place, except that it had no magic and time seemed to work differently there. In the Other Place, everyone had a counterpart, a different version of themselves—sometimes better, sometimes worse, and often about the same as they were in this place. Darius wondered if his Other Place counterpart had also been turned into a frog by a witch.

Reginald croaked with a froggy grin, "Many of us visit the Other Place to hear the music. Tonight you will hear it with us!"

When the moon rose, many of the frogs set out swimming to what seemed like the bottom of the pond. It seemed like they were about to reach the bottom, and then Darius found himself suddenly swimming upward, toward the light of the moon. When his head breached the surface, he looked around in alarm. He was in a lily pond, but there were large, tall buildings in the distance, and lots of people walked about chattering to each other. Surrounding the pond, there were tall trees, leaves in shades of gold, red, and deep orange. A large, red leaf floated near him, and he was struck by the beauty of the autumnal pond.

In the Reflection

People sat in groups all over the lawn surrounding the pond, some of them having picnic suppers in the still-warm-but-getting-crisper fall air. Tiny, glowing lights lit up the night sky, and when the music began, it was one of the most beautiful things Darius had ever heard. So beautiful, in fact, that he climbed out of the pond to get closer to the sound.

An orchestra played under an old stone arch, and a lone violinist stepped forward onto the stage. She had long, graceful arms, dark hair pulled into a ponytail in the back, and she wore a long green satin dress that matched Darius almost exactly. Mesmerized, he hopped closer. And closer. Before long, he was on the stage at her feet.

The crowd began to mumble and point at the small green creature staring at the violinist, and one man tried to reach out and catch him. Frightened, Darius hopped closer, brushing her ankle. The music stopped as she looked down and saw the frog trembling by her bare foot (she hated to wear shoes when she played). She reached down and picked him up, brought him to eye level, and smiled, placing him in the roomy pocket of her dress. Then she took up her bow and continued playing.

After the concert, when nearly everyone had gone home for the night, she walked to the lily pond and took Darius from her pocket. She lifted him up and smiled. "Don't worry, I'll return you to your home, you little music lover." She paused for a moment, then seemed resolved. "I'm just checking, mind you. You know, just to be sure. My name is Charlotte." With that, she kissed him right on his froggy mouth.

Darius felt dizzy as the spell was lifted. He stared into Charlotte's disbelieving eyes as she soundlessly held out her jacket to him, a faint blush on her cheeks. He took the jacket and kissed her hand. "I'm Darius and you've freed me from a curse."

Charlotte laughed. "I thought you liked Schubert a little more than the rest of the frogs." She hesitated for a moment. "Was this one of those 'kiss of true love' curses, like in faerie tales?" she asked. "I mean, we've only just met."

Shaking his head, grateful to have a proper neck again, Darius explained, "It was actually a kiss of good faith. That means it had to be someone who at least entertained the notion that it might work. You had to believe. And Reginald said there's no magic in the Other Place!"

Charlotte asked, "Reginald?"

In the lily pond, Darius heard Reginald's deep croak. The old bullfrog was concerned, it seemed, to leave him in the Other Place. Bending down to the water, Darius scooped the old bullfrog up in his hand and held him out to Charlotte. "Reginald, meet Charlotte."

The old frog trilled a greeting, and Darius found himself very grateful that he could still understand, even if it sounded strange to his human ears. "Reginald says he's pleased to meet you and wants to show us something."

Bending closer to the bullfrog, Charlotte peered at his green face intently. "I recognize the timbre of that croak! You've been here to listen to our concerts before!"

"Ribbit!" Reginald croaked enthusiastically.

"Does he need…?" Charlotte puckered her lips, raising her eyebrows questioningly to Darius.

At this, Darius laughed and Reginald croaked. "He says thank you, but he's truly a frog, if a magical one."

He set Reginald down by the edge of the pond and they both watched the fat bullfrog swim in a circle, causing the fallen leaves to swirl on the surface of the water. Their reflections rippled until they realized they weren't seeing their own reflections at all, but the Other Place versions of themselves. A young woman with Charlotte's face ran through a dark forest, a stringed instrument in her hand. She was out of breath, clearly running for her life. Meanwhile, a young man with Darius' face sat in a lonely, darkened tower—some type of corporate office. He was tied to his chair while two men stole paperwork and menaced him with a gun.

Charlotte and Darius blinked, and the reflections rippled and faded.

"The other 'us'—they need our help! Has all of that already happened, or is it a vision?" Charlotte inquired.

Reginald croaked, low and deep, and Darius nodded. "There's time! Charlotte, I know we've just met, but... would you fancy an adventure?"

He looked over his shoulder, but she wasn't there. He heard a loud *splash* and Charlotte was waist-deep in the pond, with Reginald swimming beside her. She hadn't heard a word he'd said.

"Darius? You are coming with us, aren't you? I mean, you're the one who can understand Reginald, and I've no idea what to tell the other-me that won't leave her thinking I'm mad!"

He joined her, wading out to swim beside them, and noting with relief that he hadn't the slightest inclination to eat the bugs that skated along the surface of the water. Together, the three of them dove beneath the surface of the pond and followed Reginald, who knew the way.

Winter

The Winterwood:
A Tale of Frost and Holly

THE WINTERWOOD WAS STILL AND WHITE. The bare branches strained against the weight of the snow, and ice decorated the twigs like tiny jewels. The whiteness was pure—no green showed, not during the winter when the Winter King ruled the Wood.

Seated upon the great Throne of Seasons, Jack Frost sighed heavily. *Nothing but white.*

Sometimes he wondered if he'd been tricked by the other fae into taking the most boring of all of the seasonal shifts in the Wood. By immortal standards, Jack was quite young. To human eyes, he appeared to be a young man of perhaps eighteen, though he had lived mere centuries compared to elder fae's millennia. His skin was pale and his hair dark. His eyes appeared to be black, but upon closer inspection, were revealed to be the dark green of pine trees at dusk. The world around him was white and still, and Jack was the kind of *bored* that only an immortal could understand.

Bianca, his white elk, nuzzled his shoulder searching him for sugar cubes.

"Fancy a ride, girl?" He scratched the soft fur between her ears, and the elk pranced at the prospect of a ride with her favorite companion.

He wasn't sure how long they'd been riding. Time was an oddly relative thing in the Wood. Jack never tired of exploration, and found Bianca as enthusiastic as he was to discover previously unknown places. Jack had been particularly lonely this winter. Few visitors had been to see him, and he couldn't leave the Wood until Gossamer arrived to take charge of Spring. Jack usually stuck around for a little while to tease her by making ice patterns on her windows in the wee hours of the morning.

A small cottage in a thicket of pines caught Jack's attention. As he moved closer, it became apparent that it wasn't so much a cottage as it was an arbor of shining green leaves and brilliant red berries. Transfixed by the contrast of the colors against the stark white snow, Jack moved forward. Bianca snuffled the leaves appreciatively.

"You on the elk! Stop! Before your beast devours my home!"

A wood nymph with hair like pale gold appeared out of what seemed like nowhere, placing herself between Jack and Bianca and the arbor.

Jack slid down from Bianca's back and smiled. "We mean you no harm. My name is Jack Frost, and Bianca and I were out for a ride. It's lonely in the Winterwood this season."

She returned his smile. "I'm Holly. Like the berries I keep."

Jack was still fascinated with the arbor of red and green. "I've never seen anything like it! Most of the other wood nymphs leave the Wood after the autumn and return in spring, taking their charges with them. But you stay throughout the winter?"

She smoothed her red cloak and replied, "I enjoy a challenge. The winter is my favorite of all of the seasons."

Holly bent down to pick up a fallen sprig from the ground and moved closer to place it through the buttonhole of Jack's coat. She laughed. "It brings out the green in your eyes."

In his heart, Jack knew he'd found the key to ending his loneliness and his boredom. He took a handful of snow and threw it at her. "It brings out the... uh... snow in your hair?" He offered a mischievous grin.

In an instant, Holly retaliated by hurling two snowballs—one of which hit Jack in the face and the other in the chest—and took refuge in the arbor. Jack gave chase and, suddenly, the prospect of another long winter in the Wood seemed bright and exciting instead of boring and lonely.

Evergreen:
A Dryad's Tale

THE FIRST TIME SHE SAW HIM, it was early November and he was wearing a red sweater. She told herself that she remembered that detail because of the way the bright color stood out against the muted winter weather, certainly not because it brought out the bright green of his eyes and the chestnut color of his hair. He'd been walking in the park, a spring in his step and a smile on his face, hand in hand with a dark-haired woman. He'd stopped at the small vending stand and purchased a cup of hot chocolate for her, though Evergreen noted that he didn't buy anything for himself. When the woman shivered slightly in the chilly breeze, he took off his green scarf and wrapped it around her neck. Evergreen watched and, for the first time in her long life, felt a stab of jealousy. Evergreen didn't miss the slight shiver that ran through his body without the protection of his scarf. She wished the dark-haired woman could see the glare Evergreen leveled at her. Her spirit form was invisible to those who lived in the physical world, but that didn't mean she didn't have an opinion.

The next time she saw him, he was again with the dark-haired woman, but Evergreen could tell the woman wasn't happy. She smiled when he was looking at her, but when his back was turned, the dark-haired woman chewed her lip worriedly, a slight frown causing a line between her eyes. He was wearing the red sweater again, and this time Evergreen noticed he wasn't wearing a coat, even though most of the other people who walked past her tree were. Again he bought a cup of hot chocolate for the woman and nothing for himself.

Nearby, a group of musicians were playing next to a blue barrel, taking donations of canned goods and cash for the poor. Evergreen had been happy when they set up a few days ago—their music was nothing like the faerie music she was accustomed to, but there was something about it that made her feel wistful in a way she'd never felt about faerie music.

Peering around the trunk of her tree, Evergreen smiled when she saw him impulsively grab his companion's hand and spin her around in time to the music. The dark-haired woman's worried expression faded as she indulged his merry mood and danced with him to the music in the park. Evergreen didn't miss that he dug into his wallet for some money to drop into the blue barrel, or the apologetic expression on his face as the small change clinked against the side.

Evergreen: A Dryad's Tale

Only a few days later, Evergreen lay on a branch of her tree, a venerable old pine that had been her responsibility for a hundred years, though the tree was much older than that. She wondered vaguely who had taken care of it before she had and made a mental note to ask Father Oak at the Yuletide gathering that would be held in a few days' time. The season's first snow had fallen the day before and her lovely old tree was blanketed in soft white.

Her heart thrilled when she caught a glimpse of red heading in her direction, but quieted in disappointment when she saw it was just a middle-aged woman in a bright holiday sweater, clutching two bags of toys as she hurried along. Evergreen went back to work, climbing to the top of her tree to inspect the bark and make certain that the old pine had the care it needed to make it through the winter comfortably.

She was nearly finished with her task when she saw something that made her jaw drop in surprise. It was the dark-haired woman, only... she was with someone else! Her pretty face did not display any of the signs of worry Evergreen had seen the last time. The woman held the other man's hand, swinging it back and forth as they hurried toward the very same vending stand where the young man in the red sweater had purchased hot chocolate for her such a short time before. The other man was taller and had blond hair instead of brown. The tall blond man wore a coat that looked new, and the woman now sported an expensive-looking scarf and matching leather gloves. He paid for two hot chocolates and some cookies as well, and they sat on a park bench to finish them off.

Evergreen found herself wondering what the young man in the red sweater was doing right now. Did he know where his companion was? Was he worried about her? Was he feeling sad? She hoped he was warm, safe, and well-fed, but something told her that might not be the case. She recalled the homeless people who sometimes slept beneath her tree or on the nearby bench, and hoped the young man was safer and warmer than that.

The couple on the bench rose and made their way toward the musicians and their blue barrel. There was no clinking of coins as the blond man in the nice coat took out a rectangular leather book and wrote something in it. He handed it to one of the singers, whose eyes widened in surprise as she looked at the piece of paper. Whatever the man had written on the paper pleased the musicians greatly, and they showed their gratitude with a lively rendition of *I Saw Three Ships*. That song had always been a source of confusion for Evergreen. What did three ships have to do with anything holiday-related, anyway? The dark-haired woman pulled on the tall man's hands, trying to get him to dance with her, and Evergreen felt a wave of righteous indignation. The nerve of her, acting like this was her idea! She was so angry that she forgot she was still touching her tree. Uncontrolled dryad magic raced from her fingers into the wood of the tree, causing a pile of snow from the widest branches—those right over the couple's heads—to fall. Evergreen didn't even try to pretend she was sorry. She lay on her branch and laughed as the perplexed couple shook snow out of their coats and, shivering, hurried away.

"Up to no good, I see?"

Startled, Evergreen jumped at the sound of the voice. A handsome sprite sat on the branch beside her, swinging his legs.

"Ghillie! I should have expected you, I suppose. You do seem to love to sneak up on me."

Ghillie didn't bother trying to look apologetic. He grinned broadly, his handsome face flushed beneath his cap of leaves. "I came to ask you something important."

"You came to see if you could sneak up on me, and you have. You wouldn't have been able to if I hadn't been… distracted."

He frowned slightly, his bluish-tinted skin flushed pinkish in the cold air. "Since when do you go around using your magic to dump snow on some mortal couple? What did they do? Try to carve their initials in a heart on your tree?"

Mutinously, Evergreen shook her head until her messy golden curls trembled. "No, it wasn't that."

"Then what was it? You know how curious I get when you're all mysterious! Come on, 'Green! What did they do to peeve you like that?"

"It was the woman. She's badly treated someone I care about. At least, I suspect she has."

"Someone you care about? Are you talking about a mortal?" Ghillie's stare was incredulous, his eyes wide.

"Yes, a mortal! There, I've explained as much as I care to. Now, what was the important question you wanted to ask me?"

She felt bad for snapping at Ghillie. He'd been a friend for a long time and sprites were terribly curious by nature.

Ghillie's bluish skin turned an odd shade, and Evergreen suppressed a giggle. Ghillie was blushing!

"Ah, I - I well…" He fidgeted nervously, tugging at the hem of his green jacket.

"Yes?"

He looked up at her with wide, hopeful eyes. "Yes? You mean you'll go? With me?"

She frowned slightly. "You haven't told me where or even asked me to go yet!"

"To the Yuletide Ball, of course! Father Oak and Lady Summer are hosting the Faerie Yule celebration, and I would very much like for you to - to attend with me."

Surprised, Evergreen stared for a moment. The Yuletide celebration happened every year and she had always gone alone. This year she hadn't given it any thought.

"I—well, I suppose that would be nice, Ghillie. Yes, I will accompany you."

The sprite gleefully tossed his hat into the air and caught it, a grin lighting up his handsome face. Without warning, he leaned forward and planted a kiss on Evergreen's cheek. Then as suddenly as he had appeared, he blinked out and away.

Startled, she pressed her hand to her cheek, but found herself picturing not Ghillie with his green-leaf hat, but the young man in the red sweater.

The next day Evergreen was just waking up her tree, getting him ready to face the day, when she heard a voice—it sounded as though someone was having a very one-sided conversation. She looked down and felt her heart begin to race at the sight of the young man who leaned his back against the trunk of her tree. He was talking into one of those small devices mortals were seldom seen without... oh, what were those things called? Phones! She crept closer, even though there was no reason to be discreet—he couldn't see her. It just seemed she should be quiet, though it made no sense. She listened.

"Hello? Angela? I was hoping to talk to Mia."

He paused and then said, "Oh. I see. Could you give her a message when she gets home? Just – just tell her Owen called, okay? Thanks. Bye."

Owen. His name was Owen. She reached out her hand as if to touch his face, momentarily forgetting she existed on a different plane. Her hand went through him as if he were a ghost.

Owen leaned back against her tree with a sigh. He seemed sad and Evergreen longed to be able to help him. He picked up his phone again and punched some numbers.

"Hi, this is Owen. I'm just wondering if you've heard from Mia? She hasn't been returning my calls and I was just hoping she's all right. Give me a call if you get my message."

Evergreen studied him closely. He once again wore the red sweater and she noticed it was a bit on the shabby side. There was a hole in the right elbow, and the cuffs were a bit rough around the edges. His tan corduroy pants were thin at the knees, and his right shoe had a small hole worn in the sole. It was more than a bit chilly and he still wore no coat. Only the green scarf helped keep out the chill. Beside him was a black case. Evergreen stared at it curiously, wondering what it was.

The phone rang, playing a few bars of a melody Evergreen recognized and was fond of—*Greensleeves*.

"Hello? Oh, hi, Mom. Fine, I'm doing just fine. How's Dad? Good, glad he's over the flu in time for the holidays. How's Denise? She did? Tell her I said she should play an unusual instrument—like the English horn, the harp, or the bagpipes. Apparently guitar players are a dime a dozen in this city. Yeah, work's hard right now. It's hard to gig when classes are in session and, well… the band broke up. Rent is due soon and Thomas ran out on me. The rat wasn't on the lease, and now I'm stuck with it. I know, Mom. I know you'd help if you could. Don't worry about it. Maybe I can find enough money for a ticket home *and* rent if I can find a decent gig… No, I haven't seen her for awhile. She hasn't returned any of my calls, and I – I think this is her way of dumping me. Oh, crap! I think I'm about to run out of minutes on my phone. I love you guys, and I'll try to get home, okay? Bye!"

Owen stuffed the phone into his pocket and leaned his head against the rough bark of the tree, oblivious to the pine sap that stuck to his hair. Evergreen watched him—she felt like she could watch him all day and never get bored. She watched as he opened the black case and took out a guitar and began to tune it. She smiled when he stood and set out a frayed-looking hat and began to strum *Greensleeves*. He played beautifully; different than the other mortals she had listened to. Where some musicians strummed chords only, Owen picked the strings with long fingers that had been well-trained. By noon, several passers-by had dropped change into

47

the hat. Evergreen's knowledge of mortal currency was shaky, but it didn't seem like a lot of money to her. By one o'clock, Owen had begun to sing while he played, and Evergreen decided he possessed the voice of an angel. She fervently hoped he would be able to earn enough money to go home to his family for the holiday.

The musicians with the blue barrel showed up around three, and Owen stopped playing to talk to them. The lead guitarist smiled at Owen. "Sounds good, man."

Owen returned the smile with a handshake. "Thanks. You guys sounded pretty sweet the other day. I'm taking a breather—been at it since this morning. I don't want to compete with the donation barrel. I'm pretty sure that's bad holiday karma. Poor kids need clothes and food a lot more than I need a plane ticket. How late do you usually play?"

The other musician smiled his appreciation. "Thanks. We're done around eight at the latest. The park isn't safe after that."

Owen packed up his guitar and picked up his hat. "Looks like enough for some ramen noodles and possibly a coffee. Good luck, you guys. It's a tough crowd."

The musician laughed. "I hear you, man! I'm Jay Byrd, and these sorry souls are Belinda, Reggie, and Jorge. Together we're Jay-bird and the Robins."

"I'm Owen. You're a band? What do you play?"

Jay sighed. "We used to do the college bar-band scene until Wicked Keen showed up earlier this year and suddenly they were all the rage and no one had the time of day for J-bird and the Robins."

Owen winced. "I've got good news for you, my friend. Wicked Keen is no more. They broke up."

One of the Robins, Jorge, let out an exuberant, "Woo-hoo!"

Jay wasn't convinced. "Are you sure? They were kings around here! The college kids couldn't get enough of them!"

"I'm sure. I was the guitarist."

Jorge grimaced guiltily, and Belinda fought the Cheshire Cat grin that had crept onto her pretty face. Jay offered a sympathetic pat on the shoulder. "We've all been there, man. You have a great sound—vocals and guitar. It'll get you somewhere eventually."

As the musicians set up to play, Evergreen heard Owen mumble, "Yeah. Somewhere, someday. Just not home for Christmas, apparently."

For the rest of the week, things followed a pattern Evergreen was starting to look forward to immensely. Owen arrived in the morning to play, left by three so the Robins could play for the charity, then came back around eight to play some more. Owen had been playing and singing for about half an hour when Ghillie showed up.

"Hi there, 'Green. You ready to dance the night away?"

Ghillie was nearly bouncing with excitement, but Evergreen was paying rapt attention to Owen, who had just begun to sing *Greensleeves* again.

"Shh! This is my favorite one!"

Ghillie glanced from Evergreen to Owen and back again. "That's the mortal, isn't it?" His tone had gone from excited to flat. When Evergreen didn't reply, he shook her shoulder gently.

"Yuletide Ball? Father Oak? Lady Summer? Remember? You said you'd come with me."

Evergreen slowly tore her attention away from Owen's music to face Ghillie. She sighed heavily. "Sorry, Ghillie. I forgot. I haven't made us late, have I?"

He shook his head. "Not yet, but if we sit here all night listening to the mortal singing and playing, we surely will be!" He took her hand, casting a worried look back at the mortal with the strange-looking lute. It didn't sound like anything compared with the faerie music he was used to, but it seemed to have Evergreen entranced.

"That song the mortal plays? It's a faerie tune. Did you know that?"

Evergreen looked back at Owen, still playing and singing under the tree. "I like it the way he plays it."

Evergreen: A Dryad's Tale

The Yuletide Ball was held in the heart of Faerie, hosted by the Great Oak King of the Free Folk, and Lady Summer, one of the Queens of Faerie. The best faerie musicians had been hired, and it could not have been brighter or more beautiful, but Evergreen felt empty. She missed the sound of Owen's voice and guitar, and she missed watching him as he played. As she danced with Ghillie, made small pleasant-talk with old friends and acquaintances, and took in the beauty of the faerie palace decorated in midwinter splendor, she grew restless. She was lost in thought—wondering if Owen would make enough money playing in the park to afford the ticket home he wanted so much—when she suddenly realized that Ghillie was trying to get her attention.

"Evergreen!"

She met his eyes and felt sorry. Poor Ghillie was trying hard to make her smile and laugh. He had probably been telling a joke or a funny story. Now as he looked at her with a hopeful expression, she had to disappoint him.

"What did you say, Ghillie? I'm sorry—my mind wandered."

He scowled, taking off his hat and spinning it nervously on his finger. "Wandered right out of Faerie and back to your tree with that caterwauling mortal and his funny-looking lute!"

Surprised at the usually-merry Ghillie's angry tone, she retorted without thinking, "At least Owen cares about something other than himself! While you've been cavorting about with the nyads and the garden faeries and the gnomes, I've been doing my job: caring for my tree. Owen isn't selfish. He barely has enough money to get by, and he still donates some of his earnings to that blue barrel every time he plays!"

Their argument was starting to draw the attention of others. A blue faerie with yellow butterfly wings gave Evergreen a disapproving glare, and a passing gnome stopped to listen, evidently concerned his people might be maligned.

Her words hit home. Ghillie's face fell. She felt bad about hurting him, but what she'd said was true. Ghillie was an irresponsible sprite whose duties were as nebulous as his whereabouts often were.

"Evergreen, I've loved you for two hundred years. I may not be as serious and serene as a dryad, but I'm no silly garden faerie. I realize you're infatuated with the mortal, but in a hundred years, he'll be long dead and I'll still be here, the same old Ghillie, waiting for you when you're ready."

Ghillie meant well, she knew that, but the casual way he mentioned that Owen would die… it hurt her tremendously to think about it. What would she do if—no, *when*—he died? For that matter, what would she do when he made enough money to go home for the holidays? Would he even come back—and if he did, would he come to the park and play by her tree? She suddenly felt foolish and afraid. The Yuletide Ball, as lovely and ethereal as it was, seemed suddenly cold and austere. She took one look at Ghillie's dear, familiar face and at the unwelcome onlookers, and ran out into the forest alone.

Dryad magic was a useful thing. Even blinded by tears, Evergreen found herself back at her tree in moments. She caressed the bark lovingly and lay face down over a branch, her feet hanging down and her head pillowed on her arms. Owen was nowhere to be seen, and really that was just as well, because she was too miserable to even want to look at him. She was in love with a mortal. A mortal who couldn't love her back because he couldn't even see her to meet her! What kind of silly creature would do such a ridiculous thing! Why, she was no better than a common garden faerie or a roving sprite!

A gentle breeze rustled her hair, and she heard a voice speak beside her.

"Why are you troubled, Evergreen? Is your tree not the loveliest in the park? His needles are bright, his bark is well-cared for, and he has grown this strong under your expert care. What brought you to leave the celebration early and your friend alone?"

Father Oak may have had the appearance of an old man, but he perched on the branch beside her with the same ease as she did.

Evergreen sat up to face the old forest guardian. "I'm sorry, I didn't mean to cause a spectacle or ruin the celebration."

The old forest guardian put a gentle hand on her shoulder. "Everyone has already forgotten. Merrymaking has since recommenced. But you haven't answered my question. Why are you so sad, my dear?"

At that moment, Evergreen saw Owen crossing the path, carrying his guitar case. Her heart thrilled, but Ghillie's words came to mind and she was staggered by the knowledge of his mortality.

Father Oak followed Evergreen's gaze, but said nothing. They sat in silence as Owen tuned his guitar and set out his hat. After Owen had completed his first song, Father Oak sighed. His breath caused a new sprig of green needles to grow where it made contact with the wood.

"You're in love with the mortal."

Evergreen nodded silently.

"Even though you know he will die?"

Again, she nodded. "I feel more alive when I listen to him play and sing than I ever have in all of my immortal life. It's like I can almost touch and smell a different kind of life. A life I wish I could have."

"If it were possible for you to become mortal yourself, you know that there's no guarantee he would also fall in love with you?"

"Yes, I understand that. But at least I would *know*."

From the new twig he had caused to grow, Father Oak plucked a small, silvery pine cone. The silver glow of his magic created a delicate chain, and the newly forged necklace hovered before Evergreen.

"Take the necklace, Evergreen. Put it on and you will become visible to the mortal. Three times you may wear the necklace and, if you are able to gain the mortal's love in return, you may choose to remain with him on the mortal plane. We of Faerie will be sad to see you go, for you are a dedicated dryad and your tree has flourished under your care." Father Oak smiled gently, raising her chin with an outstretched finger. "We would miss you, my child, but Lady Summer and I have known of your growing dilemma longer than you think. There is no crueler fate than an immortal life of sadness, so we have decided to extend to you this chance to find out if a mortal life is what you truly desire."

Below, Owen had begun to play *Greensleeves* and Father Oak remarked, "The mortal does play remarkably well. That song is a faerie song, you know."

Evergreen's hazel eyes filled—tears of happiness replaced the tears of sadness—and she impulsively threw her arms around Father Oak. "Thank you! Thank you for this chance! I just know I can make it work!"

Father Oak patted her back and whispered, "Take care, Evergreen. The mortal world can be a dangerous place."

With that, Father Oak was gone.

Evergreen stared at the silver pine cone necklace in her hand. Below, Owen still played. There was truly no time like the present. She clasped the necklace around her neck, and—

—screamed as the world blurred and the ground lurched toward her so quickly she had to be falling. Falling? What kind of dryad fell out of her own tree?

As she landed on the ground with an inelegant thump, Evergreen had just enough time to think to herself that apparently *she* must be the kind of dryad that fell out of her own tree, because that was just what she had done.

The music stopped and Evergreen found herself looking up into Owen's concerned green eyes.

"Are you all right?"

She sat up quickly, suddenly realizing she was terribly cold. Not something she was used to feeling. Owen offered her a hand and she took it, surprised at the warmth.

"Seriously, are you okay? You fell out of a tree. You could be concussed or something."

"I'm fine. I just lost my balance is all. I've never done that before, but I suppose there's a first time for everything." Evergreen looked down at her clothes, suddenly afraid she was still wearing her dryad clothing made of flowers and leaves. She was thankful to discover that Father Oak had thought of that in his enchantment. She wore the same kind of pants she saw mortals wearing around most of the time—some kind of thick material with an indigo hue. She was also wearing a bright green sweater and, for the first time in her long life, shoes.

Curiously, Owen looked up into the tree and then back at her. "What were you doing up there, anyway? I've been playing over here for a while, and I never saw anyone climb this tree."

Before she thought better of it, Evergreen said, "I was tending my tree. It's my responsibility."

Owen smiled. "So you're a gardener? Do you work for parks and rec?"

Unsure of what to say, Evergreen mumbled, "Not exactly. I was already up there when you started to play, and I didn't want to disturb you. I—" She blushed. "I really like to hear you play. *Greensleeves* is my favorite."

"Mine too. I always play that one around the holidays, but I like to sing the old words instead of the Christmas ones. Most people don't notice because they don't know the words anyway. I was just about done for the night. Usually playing warms me up pretty fast, but it's colder tonight than it has been. You're not wearing a coat or gloves or anything! If whoever you work for is going to send people out to take care of trees at night, they should at least provide you with appropriate clothing."

Evergreen wasn't sure what to say, so she didn't say anything at all. Apparently Owen liked to talk, because he just kept going. She felt her lips curving into a smile. She hadn't known that about him, but she liked it. She liked the sound of his voice.

"Anyway, since it's not every day that a pretty woman falls out of a tree practically right on top of me, would you like to get some hot chocolate? You must be freezing! Oh, I'm Owen. I guess it's probably weird to ask someone to have a hot chocolate if I haven't even introduced myself!"

"It's nice to meet you, Owen. I'm Evergreen, and I would love to have a hot chocolate with you!"

He laughed out loud. "So a gardener named Evergreen fell out of an evergreen tree? No one would believe me if I told them!"

Evergreen and Owen went to the nearby vending stand and he bought a single cup of hot chocolate. Evergreen had never tasted mortal food before and found that the hot chocolate was delicious. Noticing that Owen had once again not ordered anything for himself, she handed him the steaming cup.

"Here, have a sip yourself. You must be cold too."

He tried to protest, but she firmly pressed the cup into his hands.

"Drink."

Owen met her eyes over the cup of cocoa and smiled. "You're bossy, Evergreen."

She watched as he took a drink, her arms crossed stubbornly.

He finished and passed the cup back to her with a wink that nearly stopped her heart. "But I should tell you that I like bossy women."

They walked for a long time, hand in hand after the hot chocolate was gone, talking and laughing together. She learned that he was a student and had gone to school far from his home because he had auditioned for a band and made the cut. The band was called Wicked Keen. Owen had been the lead guitarist, but when the band broke up, he'd been left with more bills than he could reasonably manage and a school schedule that made it difficult to get a regular job. He told her about Mia, the woman he'd been seeing, who'd dumped him for a former bandmate he'd previously considered a friend. He told her about his family: His father had been sick recently, but was feeling much better, and he had a little sister named Denise who wanted to be a musician as well. In fact, Owen was *still* telling her things when Evergreen felt an odd magical tug from the silver pine cone around her neck. It must have been warning her that it was time to return to her tree for the night.

Somewhere a clock chimed midnight, and Owen stopped talking. "It's late, Evergreen. May I walk you home?"

She nearly panicked. How could she explain to him that she lived in a tree and would probably be fading into invisibility at any given moment?

She managed to stammer, "I - I'm actually very close to home right now. It'll only take me a moment to get there. I've enjoyed this evening very much, Owen."

"Me too. I'll be playing again tomorrow night. If you care to stop by, we could make another evening of it. I know of an especially fine hot chocolate establishment in the area. I can give you music and a hot drink—that is, if I make enough playing tomorrow to fund the hot drink. Would you care to spend another evening with a poor musician?"

Her smile felt as though it had exceeded the boundaries of her face. "That sounds like a lovely evening. I'll be there with bells on!"

As they parted ways, Evergreen felt her dryad magic begin to pull her back toward her tree. She disappeared, fading from the mortal world. Possessed by a sudden, mischievous urge, Owen gathered a handful of snow and turned around to toss it at her back, but the snowball fell with a soft thump—she was gone.

Evergreen: A Dryad's Tale

―――― ◇ ――――

Back at her tree and back in her faerie form, Evergreen went about settling her tree for the night, all the while smiling and singing to herself.

Greensleeves was all my joy
Greensleeves was my delight,
Greensleeves was my heart of gold,
And who but my lady greensleeves.

She placed the silver pine cone necklace in her pocket and tried to contain her excitement until she could see him again the following night.

―――― ◇ ――――

The next night, Evergreen was a bit wiser. She exited her tree before putting the necklace on and then sat down beneath the pine to wait for Owen. Once again, the enchantment had placed her in human clothing: this time a long brown velvet skirt, a sweater that reminded her of the moss that sometimes grew on the north side of her tree, and tall brown boots that protected her flesh from the cold. She wiggled her toes inside the boots and found that—while they weren't something she was used to wearing—they were quite comfortable. She saw him approaching at a slight distance and her heart soared.

When he arrived, she let him pull her to her feet and returned his enthusiastic, "Hi!"

He unpacked his guitar and began tuning the strings. "I was half-convinced you weren't real. I mean, a beautiful gardener falls out of a tree at my feet, shares a cup of hot chocolate, and then disappears into the swirling snow at midnight? A bit dramatic, don't you think?"

Truthfully, Evergreen replied, "It was magic."

Cheerfully, Owen agreed. "I thought so, too. I'm glad you showed up again. Say, can you sing?"

She could sing faerie music, but then again, all the inhabitants of Faerie could sing those songs. She'd never tried to sing any mortal music, though she was starting to feel as though she very much wanted to give it a try.

"I don't know a lot of the words, but I do know *Greensleeves*. I'm more than willing to give it a try if you want me to."

So it was that Evergreen spent the first part of her evening learning the words and tunes to human Christmas songs. Although she still considered *Greensleeves* to be her favorite, there were many others she enjoyed as well. Owen seemed to like the way she sounded when she sang, and so did many of the passers-by. More people than usual stopped by, dropping change and small bills into Owen's frayed hat.

She had such a good time singing with Owen and his guitar that the time flew and before long it was after ten-thirty. She reached up to tug at her necklace, giving it a mental admonishment that it had best hold out until at least a *bit* after midnight.

This time, as Owen counted out the money in the hat, his face broke into a smile. "Hey, a couple more nights like this and I might be able to get a ticket home for Christmas!" He looked up suddenly, as if something had just occurred to him. "You should get some of this. After all, I think it was you that pulled them in. Your voice is amazing!"

Evergreen politely refused to accept compensation and remained firm, stating that if he wanted to pay her for singing with him, he should just buy her a cup of hot chocolate instead. He tried to protest, but gracefully caved rather than argue further.

Once again, they headed for the small vending stand, and once again they shared a single cup of cocoa; but this time, Owen didn't want to talk about himself. He wanted to know about her. They sat on a park bench, and Evergreen did her best to answer with as much truth a possible, without saying anything that would cause him to discount her as a lunatic.

When he asked, "Have you always lived here in the city?"

She offered weakly, "For a long time, anyway."

Eventually, she managed to turn the conversation back to more comfortable topics like music and Owen's plans for the Christmas holidays, should he manage to make enough money to purchase the ticket.

Even though it was late, there was music in the air this close to Christmas, floating into the park from a nearby restaurant. Something about the music and the crisp cold of the night air filled Evergreen with a spirit of playfulness. Impulsively, she pulled Owen to his feet, dancing him around the way she'd seen him dance with the dark-haired woman so many days ago. He took over the lead, whirling her around and catching her before she could topple from dizziness. When the song ended, they landed in the snow in a tangled heap, laughing. They stood, brushing snow off of themselves and each other, and before Evergreen knew what was happening, Owen had his arms around her and his lips against hers. It was a quick kiss, but she had never felt so happy in her long, long life.

To her amusement, Owen was blushing. "I - I know we've only known each other for two days, but it really seems like much longer. I hope you're not offended?"

Laughing, she took his hand and wrapped his arm around her shoulders. "I'm not offended, I'm happy. I'm so glad to have met you, Owen. You really have no idea how very happy you've made me."

Just when they were about to kiss again, the clock began to chime midnight, and she once again felt the magical tug from the silver pine cone. Sighing, she said, "I have to go. Same time tomorrow night?"

A grin lighting up his face, Owen replied, "I wouldn't miss it for anything!" He scooped up a handful of snow and tossed it at her, and this time she had time to retaliate. She aimed for his head, and as he was laughing and wiping snow from his face, she crossed over into Faerie and disappeared from the mortal world for the second night in a row.

Ghillie was waiting for her when she returned, still humming to herself. The blue sprite had his hands jammed into the pockets of his leafy suit jacket, and a downcast expression on his handsome face.

"I heard you singing with the mortal."

She sat down beside him on the branch. "How did we sound?"

"Beautiful. You sounded beautiful together. Father Oak told me about the - the deal he made with you. Are you going to choose mortality for the human?"

She nodded her affirmation, expecting an angry outburst from her friend who wanted to be more. He surprised her with a hug instead.

"Then I want you to know that I'll take care of your tree for you when you've gone, and I'll always be here, even if you won't be able to see me anymore. So, if you come to sing here with your human, even if no one else comes to listen, I'll be here. Play me a round of *Greensleeves* around Yuletide and I'll be clapping my hands and dancing about like a silly garden faerie." The blue sprite planted a gentle kiss on her forehead. "I want you to be happy, 'Green. I saw you with him, and you were happier than I've ever seen you. You have my blessing." He muttered as an afterthought, "As though you need it."

Her eyes shining with tears that were mostly happy—but somewhat bittersweet, knowing she would never see Ghillie again if she became mortal—she replied, "I may not need it, but that doesn't mean it isn't wonderful to have it. Thank you, Ghillie. You're a dear friend."

He dashed the tears from his cheeks as though their very presence offended him. "Don't I know it."

Her decision made, Evergreen went about the business of making her tree comfortable for the night one last time. She explained to the dear creature that she would be going away, but would visit from time to time, and that Ghillie would be caring for him in her absence. The venerable old tree did not seem perturbed by this, and Evergreen was relieved her departure wouldn't cause her tree to feel abandoned.

She could scarcely wait until the next evening, but when it finally started to get darker outside, she again climbed down from her tree, giving its bark a quick kiss for luck. She fastened the silver pine cone necklace, and felt the odd thrill of transformation as she changed for the last time from an ethereal green-skinned dryad, clad in leaves and flowers, into a young mortal woman with blond curls, pale skin, and hazel eyes. She found she wore a long green dress made of warm material and the same brown boots she'd worn the day before. She leaned against the tree, waiting for Owen to appear, but he didn't come. She waited until the big clock chimed nine times, and then she began to worry. What if he'd decided not to come? What if he'd changed his mind about her? What if he'd made enough money and bought that ticket home? What if—she shuddered at the thought. What if something had happened to him? She remembered the band with the blue barrel, one of them saying something about the park not being safe at night…

Evergreen had had enough of standing around waiting. She had to find out where Owen was, needed to know that he was all right. First, she made her way over to the vending stand. The shopkeeper hadn't seen Owen that night, hadn't seen him since the previous night when he'd purchased the cup of cocoa to share with Evergreen.

Nearby, Jay Byrd and the Robins were setting up to play. Evergreen ran up to them, breathless with the cold and exertion.

"Have any of you seen Owen? He - he plays here in the park, and we were supposed to meet, but he's terribly late, you see, and the park isn't always safe at night."

Jay frowned. "I warned the boy. You're the woman who sang with him last night, aren't you? Were you two supposed to gig together again tonight?"

Evergreen nodded. "He said he would be here, right by my—by the tree, but—" She waved a hand toward the old pine that had no Owen beneath its branches.

"Isn't it possible he just forgot, or woke up with a cold or something? Why don't you just call him?" Reggie asked.

"I don't have a… phone. We haven't known each other long, I just - I just feel like something is wrong!"

Belinda slipped an arm around her shoulders and offered her the cup of hot tea she'd been sipping from. "Come on. You're freezing!"

As Evergreen dutifully drank, she was grateful for the kindness and warmth.

"We'll have a look around the park, just to be on the safe side," Jay stated. "There are a lot of hidden places and shortcut paths. If Owen was trying to get home with his earnings, he might have tried a lesser-used path. Jorge, Reggie—take the western gate near the play area. Check the wooded path by the farmer's market area, would you?"

The two men agreed and headed off. "Belinda, stay with the barrel and call if Owen shows up over here."

She pulled her phone from her pocket and nodded her agreement. "Full bars. I'm good."

Jay stayed on the same side of the park as Evergreen, but they split up to cover more ground.

She wasn't familiar with the park, save the parts she'd been able to observe from her tree, but she was determined to find Owen and was becoming more and more convinced that something had happened to him. A flash of bright green from behind a shrub caught her attention. There in the snow, half-covered by the shrub, was Owen's guitar, broken. Fear bubbled up inside her like a wild, terrified beast, and she had to fight to keep calm. The snow was covered in footprints and the clear signs of a scuffle. Owen's green scarf lay near the broken guitar. She picked up the scarf and wrapped it around her neck and body, shivering in the cold. Her mortal body was so much more fragile than her faerie one!

Desperately, she glanced around for any sign of Owen and felt her heart nearly stop when she saw a patch of red against the snow near a small stand of fir trees. She knew without doubt it was the red of his sweater. She ran to him as fast as her mortal legs could carry her, sliding to a stop in the snow beside him. Owen lay on his back, a bruise forming under his right eye. He was unconscious, his skin as cold as ice.

"Owen! Owen, you have to open your eyes! It's me, it's Evergreen! We - we had plans for the evening, so you just have to wake up!"

His eyes didn't open, but he muttered deliriously, "Evergreen... need to find Evergreen..."

She felt as if her heart would explode. She tried to pull him into a sitting position, but he was too heavy for her to make much headway. What kind of world was this, where a person could wait two hundred years to find love, only to lose it because of some careless thief?

Quickly, she removed the scarf and wrapped it around as much of him as it could reach. Rocking back and forth, hoping that the motion might cause him to wake, she sang,

> *Alas, my love, you do me wrong,*
> *To cast me off discourteously.*
> *For I have loved you well and long,*
> *Delighting in your company.*
> *Your vows you've broken, like my heart,*
> *Oh, why did you so enrapture me?*
> *Now I remain in a world apart*
> *But my heart remains in captivity.*

"Owen, you have to wake up! Do you know what I've done? What I did for the love of you? I'm no mortal woman, not by nature! It's magic that has made me thus! I'm a dryad, a tree-guardian from the Faerie realm. I fell in love with you, watching you play and sing by my tree, and - and I became mortal so I could be with you!" She shook him, harder than maybe she should have, but desperation was filling her very heart as his skin grew colder and colder.

"Help! Someone help us! Is anyone here who can help us? Jay! Belinda! Can anyone hear me?"

There was no one near enough to see them or hear her cries for help. She had ventured off the path to find Owen, and the small vending stand was far enough away that there was no way the man inside could hear her shouts. Somewhere in the distance, the clock chimed ten o'clock, and her sense of urgency was compounded. In her mortal form, she had no magic to help him, but if she used the necklace to turn back into a dryad… she would be able to save his life. She suddenly felt terribly calm. She knew what to do, how to save his life, and that was all that mattered.

Taking the small silver pine cone from around her neck, she felt the tug of magic as she turned into a dryad again. Taking the silver pine cone in her hands, she pressed it against Owen's cold hand. He was so close to death that, even in her faerie form, she could barely detect a breath— but breath there was, and it was all she needed. What she intended to do would cost her dearly, but hadn't Father Oak said there was truly nothing crueler than an immortal life of unhappiness? Without Owen, she would be unhappy. So it was with no further thought that Evergreen called upon the essence of her dryad power, her very own life force, to summon him back from the brink. The knowledge that she wouldn't be able to share a life with him paled in comparison to her need to fight back his death. The two figures in the snow were enveloped in a soft green light, like the needles of a pine tree against the white snow of winter. The light grew, finishing in a brilliant flash. When the light had faded, there was only one figure lying in the white snow. Owen sat up suddenly with a gasp, clutching the green scarf to his chest as he looked around in alarm.

"Evergreen? Evergreen, I - I thought—" He looked in bewilderment at the set of footprints that ended where he sat in the snow, recognizing the smaller footprints of a woman's shoe. There were no footprints leading away from him, and Evergreen was nowhere to be seen. He reached out to pick up something shining on the ground, and stared at the object he now held in his hand. Evergreen's silver necklace with the silver pine cone charm. He held a hand to his head as he staggered to his feet. He'd been attacked by muggers who'd stolen all of his money and bashed him over the head with his own guitar before leaving him for dead. He remembered worrying they'd find Evergreen waiting for him by the tree and do her harm. Now he was just confused.

"Are you looking for someone, my boy?"

An old man was standing right beside him. Owen's confusion increased exponentially. There were *no* footprints anywhere near the old man. It was thought his feet weren't touching the ground.

"How did you—I mean, I'm sorry, sir. How did you get here, and did you happen to see a young woman with blond hair? I know she was here." He held out his hand to display the silver necklace.

The old man touched his hand to Owen's head, and the young musician felt warmth pulse through his freezing limbs. A terrible thought came to mind.

"Am I dead? Is - is this the afterlife? Are you - are you God? Or an angel or something?"

Father Oak laughed softly. "I am not an angel or a god. And you are not dead, I assure you. Evergreen saved your life." The old man's expression grew sorrowful as he took the silver necklace from Owen's hand. "I never intended this gift to cause her such grief. I meant my gift to provide her with an opportunity to make up her mind. And she had. She had chosen to remain a mortal to be with you."

"A mortal? What - what do you mean?"

Father Oak shook his head. "Evergreen was a dryad. The tree in the park was hers to look after, and it was from her tree that she fell in love with you from afar."

Owen's eyes widened. "A dryad? A tree guardian? I - I thought she was a gardener. For parks and rec," he finished lamely.

"She was a dedicated guardian of that old pine near where you play and sing. And now I fear she may be gone. You see, she gave up her chance for a mortal life with you to save your life as you lay dying in the snow. She's hardly moving."

Owen looked around, unable to see anything at all. "She's not even here! How do you know whether she's moving or not?"

The old man handed the necklace back to Owen. "She's lying right there, in her faerie form. You cannot see her because you exist in the mortal world and she is on the brink of death in Faerie."

Frowning, Owen argued, "But how can I see you, if you're in Faerie and so is she?"

"Magic. I possess stronger magic as the Great Oak King than most of the inhabitants of Faerie put together. And now I am going to need your help to save Evergreen's life."

"Anything, I'll do anything! I've never met anyone like her. I - I think I love her."

A childlike grin lit the old Oak King's face. "Just the words I needed to hear, my boy. Now, take the silver pine cone and kneel down in the snow, right there—no, to the left a bit—there!"

Owen did as the old man asked.

"Now, take the pine cone and hold it out in front of you. Hold it out until I say to stop, no matter how bright the light, do you understand?"

He nodded and held out the sliver trinket. Brilliant white light surrounded them and Owen felt scared, but not of the magic or of the old man. He was scared for Evergreen. Slowly, the magical light lessened and he could see her, lying in the snow just as he must have been himself before she rescued him. She wore a long green dress and brown boots, her blond curls damp from the snow. He held out the silver pine cone, his arms feeling like lead, and he suddenly understood that it wasn't the trinket that was heavy—it was the weight of what it represented and the incredible amount of magic it was conducting.

The old man gave Owen a long, appraising look. "I've done what I can. The rest will be up to you. She's alive, and she is mortal now. Her sacrifice was not in vain, I can tell that by looking at you, Owen."

Somehow Owen knew in his heart that the old man was not just looking *at* him, but somehow looking *into* him, as though he had seen and judged what was in his heart and had not found him wanting. He felt... honored.

Evergreen stirred, opening her eyes. When she saw Owen looking down in concern, she sat up quickly.

"Owen! You're alive!" She threw her arms around him, hugging him tightly. She stopped, looking at her own hand in wonder. "*I'm* alive! We're both alive and I'm mortal, just like I wanted to be—" She looked around, sure she'd seen Father Oak only moments before.

"Where did—"

"The Oak King saved your life after you saved mine. He was just here!"

The old man was gone, but the two young people made their way shakily to their feet. The silver pine cone was still clutched tightly in Owen's hand. Evergreen allowed him to fasten it for her. The magic was gone, but it would serve as a reminder of her old life as a dryad—of her tree, of Father Oak, Lady Summer, and Ghillie, who would tend her tree in her place. Owen pulled her close and planted a kiss on her forehead.

"So… you were a dryad? And here I thought I'd fallen for a gardener!"

She smiled back at him. "It sounds like a job I might be good at. Though, I do like singing quite a bit."

He squeezed her hand as they made their way back to the path. "We can check the papers to see if parks and rec is hiring."

At that moment, Jay ran into the clearing, breathing hard. He took in Owen's rumpled appearance, broken guitar, and the bruise on his head, and moved to offer a supportive arm to the younger man. He looked apologetically at Evergreen.

"I heard you scream, but I had gotten too far away! Are you all right? Do I need to call an ambulance?"

His phone was in his hand and he was poised to dial. "At the very least, we have to call the cops and report this. If we let this slide, the park won't be safe for anyone soon enough!" He took the remains of Owen's guitar, cradling it like a child. "Sorry about your instrument, kid. You got a backup?"

Owen shook his head, for once at a loss for words. Jay called his band members to call off the search, and gave Owen's shoulder a squeeze. "The cops are meeting us up by the tree in a few." He cast a sorrowful glance at the ruined instrument and muttered, "Take your time, kid. Traffic is awful, anyway. It'll take them a bit to get here."

As they picked up the remains of Owen's broken guitar, Evergreen sadly brushed her hand across the splintered wood. "The vandals took your money for your ticket home, didn't they?"

Owen shrugged. "It doesn't matter. What's important is that we're both alive and we have each other. We can make more money—hey, what's that?" He put his hand in the pocket of his snow-soaked corduroys and drew out a small pouch. He pulled the drawstring and his eyes widened in surprise at the sight of several glittering pieces of gold. Evergreen pulled a similar pouch out of her own pocket and laughed out loud in merriment.

"Father Oak! He gave us enough faerie gold to—well, I'm not sure how far it goes in mortal terms, but it's rather a lot in Faerie. He must have bribed the leprechauns…"

Owen's jaw dropped in astonishment. "You mean leprechauns are real?"

She gave him a gentle push. "Is that so hard to believe?"

Shaking his head, Owen laughed, "I guess not. Oh, you have so much to tell me! Are gnomes real? How about elves? Sprites? Goblins?"

As they hurried down the path, hoping to get to the vending stand for some hot chocolate before the police arrived, Evergreen tightened her grip around Owen's arm, listening contentedly as he rattled on excitedly about the possible inhabitants of Faerie. She had never, ever been happier.

"Did you know that *Greensleeves* is a faerie song?"

About the Author

SARA GOODWIN does a lot of things. She once found cool Etruscan artifacts on an archaeological dig. Another time, she took a giant beetle to the side of the head on a hike and screamed bloody murder. She loves cats and takes it a bit personally when a cat is immune to her charms. She loves attending conventions, often cosplaying various characters while making and selling jewelry. She's trying to get a Ph.D. for some reason. Somehow, she found the time to write some fiction. Please enjoy the heck out of that.

@SoSaidSara

@SoSaidSara

@SoSaidSara

Made in the USA
Middletown, DE
07 June 2022